My Life Begins!

My Life Begins!

Patricia MacLachlan

illustrated by Daniel Miyares

KATHERINE TEGEN BOOKS
An Imprint of HarperCollins Publishers

Katherine Tegen Books is an imprint of HarperCollins Publishers.

My Life Begins!
Text copyright © 2022 by Patricia MacLachlan
Illustrations copyright © 2022 by Daniel Miyares
All rights reserved. Printed in the United States of America.

Library of Congress Control Number: 2021953557
ISBN 978-0-06-311601-6

Typography by Molly Fehr
22 23 24 25 26 PC/LSCH 10 9 8 7 6 5 4 3 2 1
❖
First Edition

For my grandsons, Nicky and Harry,

with my love.

—P. M.

Wishes—
Sometimes what we don't wish for
leads us to things we want.

1.

"The Trips"

I am nine years old when my life begins. Before then I was the only child. The son of Maeve and Daniel Black.

My baby picture hangs on the large living room wall all by itself. My name, "Jacob," is printed in the margin below my face.

"I look lonely," I say.

"I think 'serious' is the word, Jacob,"

says my father. "Or 'solemn.'"

I don't like either word.

"We need more happy pictures," I say.

"My friend Bella's dog has a litter of puppies. Maybe we can get puppies."

"Soon we'll have babies," says Mother. "Remember?"

"Not puppies," I say.

"Not now," says Father. "Soon we'll have happy faces."

"Very soon," says Mother, looking tired and big.

"But the babies will be *yours*," I say. "Maybe *one puppy*?"

No one answers me.

Then one day it happens. The Trips are born. That's my name for the triplets—Charlotte, Katherine, and Elizabeth.

They will soon become—

"Char,"

"Kath,"

"Liz."

It's a little like a litter of puppies.

I write in my notebook:

"A Litter of Trips"

The Trips are here.

They're not pretty.

They look like birds without feathers.

Puppies are cuter.

—Jacob

I am only nine, remember. But I can tell right away that it will be my job to study and train the Trips. My mother and father are too tired for that.

Their first months—days and nights—are full of sleep and waking to feed the Trips with sterilized bottles of formula and Mother's milk. And constant diaper changing—the diapers are the size of party napkins.

"Puppies would be easier," I say to Father.

"True," he says, yawning.

The kitchen is full of bottles. Sometimes I have to search for apples, oranges, bread, or milk for my cereal.

Father puts a small refrigerator for me in the pantry. I can find my milk, juice, snacks, and ice cream. The pantry is mine. I don't mind. It's out of the way.

More than once I find Father in there, just leaning against the counter in the quiet.

I lean against the counter too.

"I'd like a puppy," I say.

"Yes," says Father.

"Yes I can *have* one?"

"Yes, I know you want one," he says wearily.

The Trips are identical, so Mother dresses them in separate colors to tell them apart:

blue for Char,

red for Kath,

yellow for Liz.

They wear tiny bracelets with the same colors as their names. That seems strangely sad to me. After all, they've been curled up together inside my mother for months.

When my friends Allie and Thomas come to my house they are startled.

"What are those, Jacob?" Thomas asks, pointing to the beds. Thomas always asks questions when he knows the answers. He

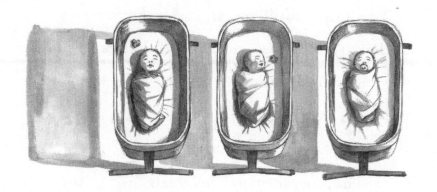

once explained to me that it gives him time to think.

"My litter of puppies," I say.

Thomas ignores my joke.

"Three," Thomas says, staring at them.

"Triplets," I say.

"They are all the same," says Allie.

She means "identical."

"They *look* the same," I say. "Mother says they'll change."

Thomas touches Liz's hand very gently. Her hand curls tightly around one of his fingers.

"Liz seems to be the most responsive one now," I say.

"Wow," says Thomas under his breath, already charmed by Liz.

I don't tell him that I'd read it is a reflex, not because she is charmed by him too. But who knows? I am just starting my study of the Trips. I am a beginning scientist.

"What do they do?" asks Allie, looking at them as if they are a science project.

They are a science project, of course. *Mine.*

"What you see is what they do for now," I say. "Except for crying, bottles, spitting up, wet diapers. And worse," I add to shock Allie.

She steps back as if the worst might happen right there in front of her.

Allie repeats what Thomas has said. "Wow."

I smile.

The Trips' first visit is over.

"Wow" is Thomas's and Allie's word for it.

———

It is a moonlit night. I hear a baby crying.

I get up and look in at my parents. They are fast asleep.

I go into the nursery, where the Trips sleep.

It is yellow Liz. She stops crying to look up at me. I pick her up.

I know how to do this. I can warm a bottle. I can change a diaper.

Her diaper is dry. Liz doesn't want a bottle. She wants to look at me. Her eyes are a dark color I can't name.

She watches me in the moonlight.

I sing her "All the Pretty Little Horses" and she is very still, listening the way she does when Father sings to her.

I touch her hand, and she curls it around my finger the way she had with Thomas. And suddenly she smiles.

She smiles!

I am right—she is the most friendly Trip so far. I also know the smile may be just a reflex. But it's still a smile.

I stand there for a while until her eyes close, and I put her back in her bed.

I cover her with the yellow blanket.

My father stands in the doorway, watching me.

"Lizzie just wanted company," I whisper.

"I love it when you call her Lizzie," he says softly.

We walk back to my bedroom.

"And she smiled!" I say, looking up at him.

"I remember when you first smiled at me," says Father. "I got tears in my eyes. I could see your future in you."

"I don't see Lizzie's future," I say.

"You will soon," says Father.

I get back into bed, and Father pulls the covers over me the way I pulled the blanket over Liz.

"This is not like a litter of puppies," I say.

"Not yet," he whispers. He touches my cheek and goes back to bed.

I watch the moonlight, thinking that I might have tears too. Like my father.

But I smile instead.

I smile. Like Lizzie.

2.

Futures

My school class is learning how to do research. Our teacher, Mr. Kelly, hands out research notebooks to all of us.

"Choose something that interests you—something you want to know more about," says Mr. Kelly. "Or a subject that is surprising and new," he adds. "The note-books are for your notes."

My friend Thomas will study the migra-tion of hummingbirds that come back to his feeders every spring.

Allie is researching her aunt who was a spy in France.

I think about writing about the growth of a litter of puppies. But I've already started my research.

My topic is: "A Litter of Trips—From Birth On."

Mr. Kelly laughs when he reads my topic title written on the first page of my notebook.

Our projects are due the last two weeks of school. Lots of time to study the Trips.

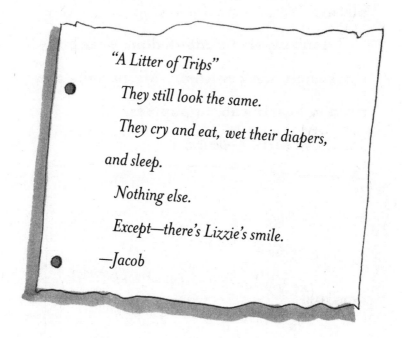

"A Litter of Trips"
They still look the same.
They cry and eat, wet their diapers, and sleep.
Nothing else.
Except—there's Lizzie's smile.
—Jacob

My mother will be glad the cold weather is over. She points to the tiny winter buntings—blue, red, yellow—and mittens and warm hats. "So much stuff!" she complains.

I don't say that puppies don't wear buntings, hats, and mittens. My parents are tired of hearing about puppies.

They're tired—*period*.

"The Trips"

Surprise—

The Trips are changing quickly. Every day.

They all have eyes turning muddy blue.

They all have their own ways of getting

attention.

Char waves her hands in the air—
Kath calls "ba ba ba"—
Lizzie quietly takes my hands.
They are all getting dark hair,
a bit curled—not yet wild like my mother's.
—Jacob

"I think their hair will soon be out of control," I tell Mother.

She laughs a long time.

Kath, in a bouncy seat, begins imitating the sound of Mother.

19

"Ba, da, ba, ba!"

Char waves her arms, excited.

That makes Mother laugh more, the two sounding wild together.

"Kath's the raucous one," I say.

"It seems so," she says. "Did you mean their hair will be like mine?" Mother asks, grinning.

It's true. Mother has to "calm her hair down" every morning—her words.

Father goes back to work. He's the principal of a middle school. The first day back he falls asleep at his desk.

"It *was so quiet and peaceful* there," he tells us, making Mother laugh. "My assistant, Jim, joked that the school ran even better when I was sleeping!

"The school nurse was sympathetic. She had twins herself. '*Only* twins?!' I said to her," says Father. This makes Mother laugh more.

Mother has taken a long time off from teaching preschool children.

"Aren't you tired of being with children all the time?" I ask. "Teaching, and now the Trips? Wouldn't you want to talk to a mature person?"

"I *am* right now," says Mother, smiling at me. "I've got you, Jacob."

Our house is filled with "Trip equipment," as Father puts it.

Three single strollers, one double,

and a triple, depending on what we need.
And special containers to carry bottles
and diapers.

Three car seats—

Three bouncy seats—

Two large playpens—

And toys—rings to chew on, rattles, and
colorful balls that they drop for us to pick
up again and again.

Julie, a photographer friend of Mother's,
comes to photograph the Trips. We call
Julie "Holy Moly" because that's what she
says all the time.

When she sees the Trips she says it.
"Holy Moly! There *are* three of them!"

She takes out her camera and takes many pictures, one after the other, as if she is snapping photos of movie stars. She makes noises to attract the Trips.

"Move close to them, Jacob. You should be in the pictures too."

Lizzie smiles and puts her hand on my cheek.

Kath's chant has become "la, la, la," in a loud voice.

"Holy Moly, they're cute," says Julie.

She sits in front of Char, who is the quiet one. Char pulls a baby blanket over her face and peeks around it.

"That will be a great picture," says Julie. "She's the shy one. Right?"

"Or the shy *sly* one," I say. "Shy Sly Char." Mother smiles at me.

"True," she says. "Sometimes she hides her face under my chin when I hold her. But she always finds a way to peek at me."

"Holy Moly, I've loved this! I'll send you the photos. My present to you," says Julie.

And Holy Moly is out the door.

The Trips stare at the door as if hoping she might burst in again to entertain them.

Two weeks later a large package arrives. Holy Moly has sent a dozen photographs of the Trips. And she has framed four.

Mother and Father and I look at them,
one after the other—

Kath, excited, with a grin, her arms in
the air—

Char, peeking around the baby blanket, looking as if she knows a secret.

Lizzie with her wise smile, reaching
over to me.

"I see their futures in their faces now," I say.

"And yours," Father says to me. He hands me another framed photograph.

A surprise. *Me smiling.*

"The Trips"

A photograph of me—

Lizzie's hand touching my face.

Not the lonely look of me that hangs alone.

Me surrounded by the Trips—

Me happy—

As if my life is truly beginning.

—Jacob

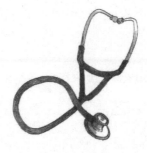

3.

"Three Dolls"

It's doctor checkup day for the Trips. We carry them out to the car.

"Will they get shots?" I ask.

Mother nods.

"Kath won't like that," I say.

Father nods.

"Kath doesn't like change," he says as he kisses the Trips, one by one, and packs them in their car seats.

I sit in the wayback seat and take out my research notebook.

I have written:

> "The Trips"
>
> My research shows Kath becoming
>
> the "tough Trip"—a good nickname.
>
> Char is the quiet, mellow one.
>
> And Lizzie the "sweet, sly explorer," as my
>
> mother puts it.
>
> —Jacob

Mother yawns three yawns in a row as we drive off.

"I think it's time," Father says to her.

"Time for what?" she asks. She yawns again.

"Time for you to get some help for the babies. So you can go back to exercise class. To get ready for what is coming next," Father says.

"What's coming next?" I ask.

Father looks at me in his rearview mirror.

"The babies crawling. And walking. The babies running!" he says. "Unleashed!"

I take my notebook out again.

I write, "the Trips unleashed." I like the sound of it. Wild puppies. "Sounds like an explosion," I say.

Mother laughs. Father reaches over to tap her hand.

"Let's get some help," Father says softly. "And it will be good for the babies to have someone new in their lives," he says.

"Maybe," says my mother, leaning back and closing her eyes as we turn into the doctor's parking lot.

In the waiting room a small girl walks up to stare at the Trips sitting on our laps.

"Three dolls!" she announces, pointing to them. "One, two, three!"

"Three *babies*," I say to her. "One, two, three."

She frowns fiercely at me.

"Dolls!" she repeats loudly. "Three *dolls*!"

The nurses are happy to see the Trips.

"They've all gained weight, the dolls!" one nurse says, hugging the bare, rosy bodies of the Trips one at a time.

"Dolls" again. I almost say "babies" to correct her.

The Trips like Dr. Will, but Kath doesn't like her shot and sharply bops Dr. Will on his nose. It makes his eyes water as he grins.

"I didn't see *that* coming," he says.

"When will they pull themselves up in a standing position?" asks Father.

Dr. Will sighs.

"No telling. One of our own babies got

up very early," he says. "Very early for us!
My wife spends a lot of time running after
her. Full days of it!"

He peers at the Trips. "They're all
strong and very agile. This one"—he taps
Kath— "is my bet to be the first."

He pats my mother's hand.

"Good luck," he says. "And get some
help. We'll see what they're doing in one
month."

We pack up the Trips again, safe in
their car seats. And the three "dolls" sleep
all the way back home.

4.

Mimi

My mother finally gives up being the only day-after-day caretaker. She hires a helper—more than a helper!

Mimi is cheerful, smart, and French. She wears long, sparkling earrings and jeweled necklaces and bracelets. The Trips' eyes get wide when they touch them.

"La," says Lizzie, reaching up to make Mimi's earring swing.

And sometimes Mimi talks to them in French.

They learn *"oui"* and *"bonjour"* and the song "Frère Jacques" in French and English. The Trips love the ending.

"Ding, ding, dong. Ding, ding, dong."

"The Trips sound very French," says Father.

"Oui," Mother says. *"Oui* means 'yes.'"

"Be careful of your jewelry," Mother tells Mimi.

"Poof!" says Mimi. "I had five children and we were fine with my jewels. Don't you worry, lamb."

Soon all the Trips begin to say their own versions of "poof," sometimes sounding like they're spitting. And once I hear Father answer a question with a "poof."

"*Bonjour*, sweet Lizzie!" Mimi calls.

Lizzie looks up at Mimi and grins. No reflex smiles anymore.

"Poof!" she says happily, both arms in the air.

Right away Mimi is a family favorite.

She is interested in what I write about the Trips. "Remember 'poof' in your research, dear Jacob," she says to me.

I peer at her. No one has ever—ever—called me "dear Jacob."

I love that Mimi calls me that.

"I feel Mimi is *my* caretaker too," says Mother. And it seems true.

One afternoon when my father and I

come home from school together we find quiet.

We find peace.

The room looks like a painting, caught in one moment. The Trips are napping in their playpens. Char clutching a stuffed bear, Kath sleeping so soundly she doesn't move when we shut the front door. Lizzie sleeps half-curled in a baby blanket. My mother sleeps on the couch, a blanket over her.

The quiet is so surprising, Father and I don't even whisper to each other.

There is a note from Mimi.

———

All are sleeping.

It is lovely.

Enjoy the peace.

The three dolls are a joy.

—Mimi

p.s. There is a ruby bracelet lost

somewhere. I must have dropped it.

Father and I walk carefully past the playpens. Then he taps me on the shoulder and points. Next to Lizzie's curled hand is the ruby bracelet, half-hidden in her blanket. Very carefully Father leans down and picks it up.

We smile at each other.

He goes to his bedroom to lie down after his long day.

I go to my room and take out my notebook. I write:

"The Trips"

Mimi has come to us.

She has brought peace.

All is well with the "three dolls."

All is well with their mother.

—"Dear Jacob"

5.

On the Move

Thomas and Allie can't believe what they see. The Trips are crawling! It's been a few months since they last saw the Trips.

"No more little beds," says Thomas.

"Nope. Gone."

Allie watches the Trips play with toys.

"They're on the move!" she says.

"Good words for it," I say. "My father calls it 'unleashed.'"

"And they don't have their own colors anymore," Allie says.

I smile.

"No. We know who they are," I say. "They're changing all the time and are different from each other. See? Char and Kath are playing together. Lizzie is crawling over to you."

"Lizzie," Thomas says softly,

remembering. "She held my finger when I first met her."

Lizzie looks up when she hears her name.

"Poof," she says, grinning at Thomas.

"What does 'poof' mean?" asks Allie, laughing.

"That's *my* word," says Mimi, coming into the room with three small sippy cups of juice.

"This is Mimi, our friend," I say. "Thomas and Allie are visiting the Trips."

"Friend *and* caretaker of the girls," says Mimi.

She hands the Trips their cups. I smile at Mimi calling them "girls."

And I smile at Thomas and Allie as they stare at Mimi's jewels.

"She's festooned," whispers Thomas, who likes new words.

"Thomas is writing about migrating hummingbirds, and Allie is studying her French aunt who was a spy."

"Ah, you're French like me."

"Only a bit French," says Allie.

"*Un peu*," says Mimi. "A little."

"*Oui*," says Allie, making Mimi laugh.

"I knew a 'spy,' as you call it. I think the proper term is 'special agent,'" says Mimi.

"Do you ever learn secrets?" asks Allie.

"Never a one," says Mimi. "But I try."

Allie and Thomas laugh.

"It's *all* secrets," says Allie. "Hard for me to study."

"So are the hummingbirds," says Thomas. "Jacob is lucky—he can follow and watch and write about the Trips."

"And dear Jacob is very good at it," says Mimi.

Char looks up at Allie and Thomas, holding up a book.

"She wants us to read a book!" says Allie.

"Quiet. But still on the move," I say.

Allie sits down on the floor, and Thomas gathers more books. Thomas points to a picture.

"Dog," he says.

Char points to another picture.

"Tree," says Allie.

Kath and Lizzie crowd in on either side
of Thomas and Allie. Kath points.

"Bird," says Thomas.

Kath looks at the large window.

"She knows there are birds outside," I
say.

It is quiet.

And then, suddenly, the quiet is over.

The Trips crawl away again to pick up rattles and balls and pull both ends of a stuffed bear. Lizzie plays with the laces of Allie's bright red sneakers. She unties the laces, looking happy with herself.

"La!" she says, looking at Allie.

"You did it!" says Allie.

"Reading time's over," says Thomas, laughing.

"But still on the move," says Allie.

"*Oui*," says Mimi, picking up Lizzie.

"*Oui*," repeats Lizzie, surprising Mimi.

Lizzie puts her fingers on Mimi's lips—very gently—

"*Oui,*" she whispers. And I see tears in Mimi's eyes.

That night I write by lamplight:

"*The Trips*"

The Trips have their own language.
But they are quick at learning ours.
Every day we hear ourselves,
in Trip words.

—Jacob.

6.

A Sneak

The Trips see something new! They stop playing.

"Da," says Lizzie, pointing.

They stare at Father, all dressed up. He has a flower in his lapel.

Kath points to it.

"Flower," he tells her.

"Fla!" she says.

"Yes!" says Father.

"They're all talking," I say.

"In their way," Father says.

The Trips are even *more* excited to see Mother!

She has calmed her hair. She wears shoes with jeweled buckles. She wears sparkling earrings. Kath points at them.

And Mother wears a swirly dress!

"You're wearing a dress!" I say, surprised.

Mimi pokes me.

"And you think she looks beautiful," she whispers to me.

"And you look beautiful!" I say.

"Thank you, Jacob," says Mother. She twirls around.

The Trips all clap hands at the same time, a new favorite habit of theirs. Now when one claps they all clap!

"Today is a wedding day!" says Father. "We'll dance!"

And Mother and Father dance for the Trips. They turn so my mother's dress skirt

swings out around her. Once Father just saves Mother from falling into a playpen.

"Mo!" Char says when they stop.

"She wants 'more,'" I say.

Father picks up the Trips, one by one, dancing and whirling with them until they squeal happily.

"Mo, mo, mo!" the Trips call.

"Wedding time!" says Father.

Mother waves.

"Bye-bye!"

The Trips all wave in their own way, flapping their hands. And Mother and Father hurry out the door in a swirl of my mother's skirt.

"Mo," says Lizzie sadly, staring at the closed door. "Mo."

"Okay," says Mimi, looking out the window. "They're gone."

"You sound sneaky," I say.

"I *am* sneaky," says Mimi.

"We're going to *do* something sneaky together, aren't we," I say. "I can tell."

"We are. As soon as the girls nap in their bedroom cribs."

"Girls again," I say. I think for a moment.

"Did you have all baby girls in your family?" I ask.

"Girls and boys and dogs!" Mimi says happily.

"You had a dog?" I ask.

"I had a lifetime of dogs!" says Mimi. "When I was growing up I had Otis and Lula and Teddy, Owen—and later Tess and Neo."

She smiles with a faraway look. "Neo used to sleep next to me at night. I would wake up and see his eyes open right next to mine, as if he was watching over me."

"So many dogs?!" I say.

"*Oui*," says Mimi.

I sigh. "I want a puppy," I say. "I've given up on a litter of puppies."

Mimi nods.

"You know," she says, "many times

you talk to the girls as if they're a litter of puppies."

I stare at her, surprised. "I do?"

"Maybe you'll change that one day," she says. "You'll figure it out. Now! For our sneaky plan. Nap time!"

"Now?" I ask.

"*Oui*," says Mimi.

And we laugh as we hear a chorus of "*oui*" from the "girls."

I put the Trips in their cribs—one, two, three.

I take out my notebook and watch them from the half-closed bedroom door.

"The Trips"

I put the Trips in their cribs.

I watch them sit up and play.

Then Liz yawns.

And they all yawn.

Soon they will "fall into sleep," as Mimi says.

And they do.

—Jacob

Mimi is already at sneaky work in the living room. She has folded up the playpens.

"No more playpens," she says. "We'll carry them to the shed."

"But how will we keep the Trips safe and out of trouble without them?"

Mimi grins at me.

I wait. I can tell she is about to tell me her sneaky plan.

"All right," she says. "You and I are going to build a magical playground."

I stare at her.

"*In* the house?!" I ask.

She nods.

"Magical?"

"Yes. A magic playground," she repeats. "And I know how to do it. Poof!"

I follow Mimi as we carry the playpens to the shed.

Really? A "magical playground"?

7.

The Magic!

So it begins.

While Mother and Father are dancing—

While the Trips sleep—

Mimi and I begin the "magic."

"No playpens," I say. "It looks empty."

"It will be beautiful soon," says Mimi. She beckons to me. "Come."

She opens the front door. I follow her outside.

She beckons again. And I follow her to something leaning against the house, hidden in the tall bushes. A smooth yellow framed fence.

"A fence," I say. "This is it?"

"It's not *just* a fence," says Mimi.

"Where did it come from?"

"Home. I used it with my own children."

"Who carried it here from your car?"

"I did," says Mimi. "Pick up the other side."

"You mean *this* is going inside the house?" I ask.

"It's going to be magic," says Mimi.

I grin at her as we carry it inside. She grins back to me. I know this means we are now partners in the magic secret. *Whatever it is.*

"Put it by the large window so the girls can look out," says Mimi.

We lift it over to the window.

"Ready?" says Mimi with her sly smile.

I nod.

"Hold that side," Mimi says.

I do. And she pulls the other side so the fence opens out!

It grows. Now it's a large playground!

"There's a small door in it," says Mimi.

I take a breath.

"You're right. It's a playground," I say quietly. "It is!"

"And now," says Mimi, "it's time for magic."

Mimi and I go out to her car. We go back and forth, carrying wrapped bundles.

"What's inside?" I ask.

"Magic," says Mimi.

We carry in three baskets.

"Three?!" I ask.

Mimi smiles.

"Three girls. Lots of magic," she says.

We carry in colorful pillows and mats and piles of books. And more.

I look in the back seat of her car. "Blown-up balloons?!" I ask, laughing.

Mimi nods.

"I know," I say. "For the magic."

"Bring them in, please," says Mimi.

And I do, making sure to hold on to their strings so they don't fly away.

We have put all of Mimi's treasures around the playground. There is lots of color.

And surprises for the Trips.

"One more thing," says Mimi.

She opens the gate in the fence. She sets up the ladder inside. And Mimi takes off her shoes and climbs up to tie balloons to the ceiling beams. We stand and look at the playground.

"Magic," I say softly.

"Magic," she says.

And then we hear the waking sounds of

the Trips in their cribs.

"Nap time is over," I say.

And we carry the Trips to see the "magic" that is theirs.

And later, when Mother and Father come home, they open the door to see the beautiful playground—

To see the Trips inside, playing with baskets of toys, one with books, and one with dolls—

To see Char point to the garden of roses and daylilies and lilacs outside—

"Bood," says Char, pointing out the big window—

"She said 'bird!'" says my father. "She did!"

Mother cries and smiles at the same time. Father puts his arm around her.

"And look, balloons!" he says.

"Mimi hung them in the beams," I tell him.

"How did you get them up there?" Mother asks Mimi.

"I flew! Poof!" says Mimi, grinning.

"Poof!" echo all the Trips together.

Mother walks slowly around the playground, looking at all the new dolls and books.

She looks at Mimi.

"This is magic," she says. "*True* magic."

I see Mimi's joyful expression at the word "magic" from Mother.

I reach over and tap Mimi's hand.

"Magic," my mother says softly, almost in a whisper to herself. But we all hear her.

8.

Names

"The Trips"

  The Trips have no name for me.

  Why is that?

  They say "Mama" and "Da" for Father.

  They even say "Me–Me" for Mimi.

  But there's no name for me.

  Why not "Jacob"?

—Jacob

We have a day off from school for teacher meetings. I carry my notebook into the living room.

Mother has gone back to teaching pre-school part-time. Mimi spends more time with us.

"I'm glad you're here," I tell Mimi.

"Me too," says Mimi.

I smile. Mimi always says, "me too."

Lizzie repeats it. Then Char.

"Me too. Me too."

Kath, turning the pages of her book, looks up. "Me too."

Then she goes back to her book.

Mimi is unpacking new books for the Trips.

I sigh.

"Why so glum?" Mimi asks me.

I hand her my notebook. She reads it.

"The Trips call you 'Me-Me,'" I say to her. "And 'Mama' for Mother."

"Both easy words for them to say," says Mimi.

"And 'Da' for Father."

Mimi smiles at this.

"Your father loves the name 'Da,' remember?"

I remember.

"I hope they call me 'Da' forever!" he told us.

"But why not *my* name?" I ask.

Mimi thinks for a moment.

"Maybe they think you're one of them. They don't say each other's names yet either."

"Me? One of the Trips?"

Mimi nods.

"Only they know for now," says Mimi. "Until they can tell you. Or find a way to let you know."

"You know, I've been thinking about names," I tell Mimi.

"Mother's name is Maeve, but Father calls her 'May.' He's David, but she calls him 'D.'"

Mimi nods.

"The Trips have been called different names—'dolls,' for one," I say.

"The plumber said 'oh, those sweet baby-cakes!'" says Mimi with a grin.

"And you call them 'girls,'" I say.

"I do," says Mimi. "And you call them 'the Trips.'" She pauses. "As if they are a bunch of bananas," she adds. "All the same."

I stare at Mimi.

"Or!" Mimi says. She stops. Then speaks softly. "Like the litter of puppies you told me you wanted."

I look up at Mimi.

"Which they aren't, are they?" I whisper.

"You might think back—to your feelings

about how your life changed when they were born," says Mimi. "I didn't know you then."

I watch Char turning the pages of a book.

"I'll figure it out," I say. "Maybe I'll find their 'forever name.'"

Mimi puts her arms around me.

"I like that—'forever name.' And I know you will, dear Jacob," she says.

I smile up at her.

"I love that name," I say.

"Me too," says Mimi.

We smile at the echo of "me too's" from the Trips.

It's nighttime. There's a full moon.

I remember when Lizzie was just born, waking. And we stood together in the moonlight.

I open my notebook:

"The Trips"

I'm thinking about Mimi's words.

Is Mimi right?

Do the Trips think I am one of them?

Does my name "Trips" make them sound like a "bunch" of the same thing?

Like a litter of puppies?

Maybe "Trips" is not their forever name—like "Da."

Maybe my report for school will change.

Suddenly I stop writing. I close my notebook and walk to the window and stare at the moon.

Then I open my notebook. I write one more sentence.

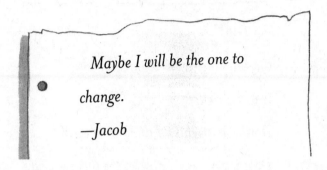

Maybe I will be the one to change.

—Jacob

I read my notebook from beginning to end. Is Mimi right? Do the Trips think I am one of them?

I think and think about a "forever" name.

But I can't find it.

9.

What Lizzie Knows

Father has started dancing with the Trips when he comes home from work.

"Still dancing," I say.

"It's my favorite exercise," he tells us. "I sometimes think of dancing down the halls of school."

"Now *that's* a pretty picture," says Mimi. "Dancing down the hallways while students peek out classroom doors!"

Mother bursts out laughing and Mimi grins. Father tries not to smile.

Mimi points to Char, Kath, and Lizzie in their playground.

"You know, the girls are changing," she says. "Would you have ever guessed that Char would become the quiet reader? She knows some of the books by heart. She knows what comes next when she turns the page."

"And Kath sets up dolls all together," says Mother. "Like a doll family."

She smiles at Father. "She even had a doll dance yesterday."

"Really?" says Father, looking surprised.

Mimi nods.

And then the something new happens!

Three ceiling balloons pop!

"Poof, poof, poof," the Trips all say, looking up.

Kath and Char go back to their dolls and books. But Lizzie crawls up to the playground fence.

She reaches high up to grab a railing. She pulls herself up. *She stands!*

"Lizzie's standing," Mother says, shocked.

"Didn't Dr. Will bet on Kath to be the first?" says Father.

We watch.

And then Lizzie turns her head and looks at me.

Me.

And I know. I know she wants me.

I quickly open the door and go over to Lizzie. I sit beside her.

"I'm here," I say softly. "She's scared. She doesn't know how to get safely down again."

I help her down and she stays in my arms, looking up at my face.

She reaches up to touch my face.

"Jay," she whispers.

My name. She whispers it, so I'm the only one who hears.

I think back to Lizzie, just born, looking up at me when I held her in the moonlight.

"How did you know that, Jacob?" asks Mother.

Father smiles at me. Maybe he remembers the night he found me holding Lizzie as she looked up at me.

"Jacob knows things," says Father.

"It's *Lizzie* who knows things," I say.

I sit with Lizzie for a long time. Long
enough for her to try to stand again—

Then drop safely into my arms again—
over and over—and over. Until she speaks
my name out loud so everyone can hear—

"Jay."

And she stands without falling.

I wake in the night. Everyone is sleeping.

I wander into the dark living room. I
switch on the light over the pictures hung
there—

me alone, looking lonely,

Julie's pictures of the lively Trips,

Char, peeking around her blanket,

Kath with her arms in the air,

And Lizzie—her hand reaching up to
touch my face as if I belong with her.

I stand there looking at the past and the
present.

And when my life began.

Then I click off the light. The moon is outside my bedroom window. My school report is almost finished. *Almost.*

"The Trips"

Lizzie showed me something today—

Of course I am one of the Trips!

I just don't know the "forever" word

for them.

The Trips is not their forever name.

—Jacob

I take a pen and cross out the word "Trips." And when I sleep that night I dream about the day the babies were born.

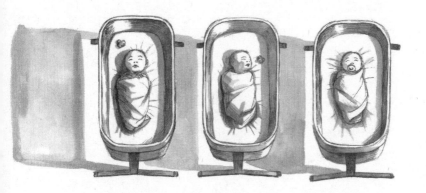

In my dream Thomas points to them in their little beds.

"What is this?" asks Thomas.

"My litter of puppies," I say.

The "forever" answer had not come to me then.

But Lizzie knows.

10.

The "Forever Name"

I wake in morning darkness. It's the day of my school report. I'm ready. Except for one last thing.

I sit in the living room alone. No Char, Kath, and Lizzie yet. No Mother and Father.

I wait, hearing the first bird sounds before daylight.

Then I hear my parents in the kitchen. They come into the living room, carrying coffee cups.

"Jacob?" Mother is surprised to see me in the half dark.

"Is something wrong?" she asks.

I shake my head.

"Isn't this your report day at school?" asks Father. "The last day of school? And your birthday!"

I nod.

"I need a favor," I say.

Father smiles and sits next to me. "What favor?" he asks me.

"I need an ending to my report," I say.

And I tell them.

Father drives us all to school—Mother, Kath, Char, and Lizzie, and me in the wayback with the strollers.

Father is grinning. He loves adventure and surprises.

"I took time off school," he says happily. "This will be fun."

"The students will miss you dancing down the hallways," says Mother, making him laugh.

"What about Mimi?" I ask. "We've taken the 'girls' away."

"I called her, Jacob," says Mother. "She'll be there when we get home. She's taking care of something today."

"What?" I ask.

"Something," repeats Father.

We turn into the school parking lot.

"We'll be in the school hallway until you want us," says Father.

"Bye-bye, Trips," I say to them.

They flap their hands. One day they'll learn to wave.

We get out. Father takes out the strollers. Mother plucks out the girls, one by one by one.

I walk to the school door and turn to watch them. I don't know why, but I feel tears in my eyes.

I go inside.

"Are you ready, Jacob?" asks Mr. Kelly.

"I am. Will you open the classroom door when I ask you?"

"Of course," he says with a smile.

We have already handed in our textbooks. "Make sure your desks are cleaned out, everyone," says Mr. Kelly.

Thomas finds a very old sandwich in his desk. We all laugh.

Mr. Kelly makes a face and points to the wastebasket.

I find my small photograph of Lizzie, Kath, and Char that I've kept there for months.

That's all.

"Now," says Mr. Kelly, "we have had many research reports from you all. Now we have the last report by Jacob. The video is turned on."

He has written the title on the black-board.

"A Litter of Trips—From Birth On."

I begin:

"I feel my life began when our triplets were born. I was kind of bored and lonely, an only child in my house."

I point to the blackboard.

"I wanted a litter of puppies. Not

triplets. Who expects *three* babies? Instead I got a litter of triplets. I'd never ever *seen* triplets. They were identical—and I called them the Trips."

I read my notebook writing to the class:

"They were not pretty. They looked like birds without feathers. Puppies would be cuter."

Everyone laughs. Even Mr. Kelly.

I take out the large pictures of them and hold them up.

"Here are Char and Kath and Lizzie," I say.

"They all look alike!" someone in the class calls.

"They did—we dressed them in their own colors.

"Blue for Char.

"Red for Kath.

"Yellow for Lizzie.

"They had bracelets with colors, as you see in this picture. But when I decided to study them I found they were different— they had different habits, different ways to let us know what they wanted.

"We got to know them. And soon they didn't have to wear their separate colors.

"I learned to warm bottles to feed them.

"I learned to change their diapers.

"I learned how they slowly yawn in the cribs and fall over into sleep.

"And I began to feel sorry calling them the Trips.

"They are more than a 'bundle of the same.'

"They are not just ONE thing called the Trips."

I walk to the blackboard and erase the words "A Litter of Trips."

"They have a new 'forever' name, as I call it."

I nod at Mr. Kelly. He smiles and opens the classroom door.

"And I have a surprise ending to my talk."

And then Mother and Father roll the girls into the room. Everyone applauds!

And the girls look up, smile, and clap too!

I walk to the blackboard and write three words there.

I write, "friends."

I write, "family."

"And meet my *sisters!*" I say as I write "sisters" on the board. "That is my 'forever' name for them!"

I walk over and take Lizzie's hand. "And the forever name for me is 'brother.'"

The class applauds and my sisters clap hands!

"You can tell they are imitators. If the class says the word 'poof,' my sisters will say it too."

The class says "poof" together, laughing, and my sisters say "poof" "poof" "poof," holding up their arms.

Everyone laughs.

"This is Char. She loves books and will be a reader."

I open a page of a book in her stroller and show it to her.

"Doo," says Char.

"That's Char's word for 'dog' so far. And Kath loves dolls. She has a family of them.

"Do you want to make the doll dance?" I ask her.

And Kath happily dances her doll around her stroller.

"My father dances," I tell the class. "She imitates him.

"And this is Lizzie, who wants to get out of her stroller."

I lift her up and she wants to stand holding on to Thomas's desk.

"Hello, Lizzie," says Thomas. She reaches down and unties his sneaker shoelace.

The class laughs and claps.

Then Lizzie takes my hand and stands for a moment. And takes three steps, holding on to my hand!

"That's the first time she's walking!" I say.

The class applauds. Even Mother and

Father applaud. And I catch Lizzie before
she falls over clapping.

"My sisters cry.

"They smile.

"They're sly.

"They're sweet.

"They're angry.

"They're clever.

"They laugh.

"And they love!

"And that's the end of my story," I say.

The class waves goodbye, and my sisters flap their hands wildly.

Everyone laughs. "They haven't learned waving yet," I say.

"The end," I say.

"And the end of school until next fall," says Mr. Kelly.

The school buses are outside. Mr. Kelly walks us to the door.

"Good job, Jacob!" he tells me.

Parents are coming to pick up their children.

"Oh!" says a woman. "Who are the wonderful babies?"

"My sisters," I say. "All three of them. And I'm their brother!"

11.

Blue Eyes

It's a short ride back home. Father is quiet, driving.

Mother turns around to look at me. "That was wonderful, Jacob. It showed where you were and where you *are*."

Father looks at me in the rearview

mirror. "I'm impressed. You were very thoughtful. And amusing."

He looks at Mother. "In fact I may not go back to work today to celebrate. Your report *and* your birthday! Both good reasons to stay home."

I lean back and close my eyes. "I'm tired," I say.

"That's because you went through months and months of the Trips' lives," says Father.

"My sisters, you mean," I say.

"Your sisters," Father repeats. And I see him smile at me in the mirror.

At home Mimi's car is in the driveway.

"Here, you take Lizzie," Father says to me. And we carry my sisters inside to their playground.

"Where's Mimi?" I ask, looking around. "You said she was taking care of something."

"Let's go outside and see," says Father, with a sly look.

He knows something.

"Wait for me!" says Mother. She knows something too.

Father opens the back door and we're outside in gardens and fenced yard.

Mimi's down the yard.

I stare.

With a puppy!

She waves at us and tosses a ball into the air. The puppy leaps and catches it.

"Good boy," says my father softly. The puppy runs up the yard with the ball and drops it in front of me. *Me!*

He is brown with dark ears. I run my hands over his warm fur.

"Whose dog is this?" I ask. "Is he yours, Mimi?"

She shakes her head. "No. I'm puppy sitting for someone," she says.

"How did it go at school today?" she asks.

"Great!" says Mother.

"Fabulous," says Father.

Mimi looks at me. "And?"

"I have *sisters*," I say. "That's their name."

"Forever?" asks Mimi.

"Forever," I say, grinning at her.

Mimi puts her arms around me. The puppy backs away a bit and makes an impatient sound.

"Toss the ball, Jacob," says Father.

"His eyes are *blue!*" I say. "Do you see?"

"I see," says Father.

"A beautiful blue," says Mother.

And I toss the ball up into the air like a fly ball. The puppy leaps up to catch it.

"Tell Jacob now," Mother says softly.

And Father does.

"Happy birthday, Jacob!" he says. "From all of us!"

The puppy drops the ball again, looking up at me.

The blue-eyed puppy is mine!

———————

My sisters love the puppy right away, pointing and smiling.

And the puppy loves them. He runs around the playground, nosing their fingers through the fence, rolling over so they can touch him.

"Doo!" says Char, pointing. She holds up a book, showing us a picture of the dog there.

"How did you find him?" I ask Father.

"A teacher friend at my school has a dog with three puppies. This was my pick."

"And mine!" says Mimi.

"And mine!" I say softly, putting my arm around the puppy.

Mother leans down to hug me. She knows I'm about to cry.

"What's his name?" I ask.

"He has no name," Father says. "He's yours to name."

"I have something for you," says Mimi. She hands me a large package.

I unwrap a large white dog bed.

"That was my favorite dog Neo's bed," says Mimi. "Remember him?"

I hug Mimi. "But wait—I remember you told me Neo slept in bed with *you*," I say.

Mother and Father laugh. The puppy licks Lizzie's hand through the fence and she laughs.

"She's laughing out loud now!" says Mother.

"He'll be a great assistant for me," says Mimi, making Mother and Father smile.

The puppy comes over to lean against me. Father takes a picture of us.

"For the living room wall," he says.

"He knows he's yours!" says Mimi. "He chose *you*. He dropped the ball at your feet when he first saw you."

"I'm his too," I say.

I pat him. His fur is mostly smooth with wavy spots. His black ears are soft. He doesn't mind when I touch them.

"He's a triplet," I say. "I could name him 'Trip.'"

But I've put that name away. Far away.

I smile.

"I name him 'Blue.' For those eyes," I say. "If his eyes change color later I won't mind. 'Blue' will remind me of the day he came to me."

I pat him. "Blue?" I say softly to him. "Do you like the name 'Blue'?"

He looks at me and falls over in my lap.

Blue.

"I have two birthday gifts for you before I go home," says Mimi. She hands me two leather-bound notebooks.

I smile at her.

"You know I'll still be writing," I say.

"I'm counting on it, dear Jacob," she says.

"I already know what I'll write," I say. "I know the titles."

I look at Father and he knows to hand

me his pen. I open one notebook and write.

"This notebook is 'Sister Stories,'" I say. "The Trips are gone."

I open the other notebook and write one word. I hand it to Father.

"Blue," he says softly.

Mimi hugs me. Father and Mother grin. Blue wags his tail. The room seems full of happiness.

Blue follows me all day: outside to play catch, to watch the birds and chase a chipmunk. He rolls in the grass so I can pet his belly.

I put the dog bed next to my bed. Father

watches from the doorway.

"This is your bed, Blue," I say. "And over here is *my* bed. Right next to you."

Blue sniffs his bed. And wags his tail.

"Blue likes his bed," I say.

"Maybe," says Father.

"What do you mean?" I ask.

He smiles.

"I think it's *you* he likes," he says.

That evening Blue and I say good night to my sisters in their cribs. They laugh as he licks their fingers through the crib bars. They all clap together and Blue whirls around for them.

I have my sisters. I have Blue.

Both.

And later that night, after Mother and Father have gone to bed, I pat Blue's dog bed. He curls up on it.

"Good night, Blue," I say.

I go to brush my teeth.

But when I go to my bedroom Blue isn't on his dog bed. He waits for me on *my* bed, wagging his tail.

I smile and think about Father's words: "It's *you* he likes."

I get into bed next to him. I pick up the notebook with his name, "Blue," written there.

Blue watches me as I write:

"Blue"
The blue-eyed puppy is mine.
My life begins again!
—Jacob

I shut my notebook. Blue nudges my hand. I pat him.

I turn off the light. Blue yawns and snuggles next to me.

And much later—in the middle of the night—I turn and see Blue's eyes looking into mine, like Mimi's dog Neo!

Blue is watching over me.

I put out my hand to pat him. And he covers my hand with his paw. And I fall back to sleep again.

My life begins again and again.